Tales from a Sick Bed

Also by L.P. Howarth published by Catnip

Bodyswap: The Boy who was 84
Tales from a Sick Bed: Fever Dreams
Tales from a Sick Bed: The Medicine Chest

Tales from a Sick Bed

Brainstorms

L. P. HOWARTH

Catnip

CATNIP BOOKS
Published by Catnip Publishing Ltd
14 Greville Street
London EC1N 8SB

This edition first published 2009
1 3 5 7 9 10 8 6 4 2

Derek Gremlin Drives & The Ghost of Christmas Shopping
© Lesley Howarth 1997
Car Sick & Stuff Police © Lesley Howarth 1998

The moral right of the author has been asserted.

A CIP catalogue record for this book is available from the British Library.

ISBN 978 1 846470 83 7

Printed in Poland

www.catnippublishing.co.uk

Contents

Never Be Afraid to Dream   7

Derek Gremlin Drives   10

Car-Sick   34

The Ghost of Christmas Shopping   56

Stuff Police   77

Never Be Afraid to Dream

You're hot – very hot. You know when you're off school and ill in bed, and everything seems kind of large and nightmarish – when your brain dips out and explores strange ideas, and the wallpaper hurts your eyes?

Eight am, and the sound of the school bus turning outside makes you feel glad you're ill. You can hear the crunch of gears, sense the rush for a scabby seat, see the driver's scowl. You drift off to sleep, and pretty soon you're in a school bus with clean seats and a smooth engine, clean air and a friendly driver . . .

Derek Gremlin turns, and his eyes are kind.

You can go wherever you want. There's a whole world out there, he says. Never be afraid to dream . . .

And the dream changes, and you're riding in the back of the Toyota with Dad's neck in front of you and the hurlsome miles unfolding ahead through what you can see between holding onto the seats. There's a moment when you think you might actually hurl on Dad's neck.

And you're pleading with them, again: "Please . . . can we stop . . . I'm really car sick?"

'Look straight ahead,' says Dad, checking you out in his mirror. 'You can't possibly be sick if you look straight ahead – it's all in the mind, you know.' He actually throws you a wink. And in that moment, you decide on – revenge.

And in the week before festivities, at last you're out of bed and downstairs, just in time for the holidays – score. The Christmas lights remind you of something. So do the headlines that night. 'Christmas Shopping Boy Dies In Hospital'. And you read the story and wonder about people missing Christmas the world over, about people having no Christmas at all, about the ghosts of all the people who ever missed Christmas pressing around you, wanting to join in and not being able to.

Wanting, perhaps, to spoil it.

And you wonder what that's like.

Start of spring term, and you call your mate Justin, but guess what, he's tidying up.

'No way. Is he all right?'

'He went down the dump,' his dad says. 'He came home looking kind of grey, and he's been tidying the house ever since.'

This is huge. It's humungous. Normally he's so untidy, there's bracket fungus growing under his bed. When you go round and see him, he blanks you.

'Jus,' you insist, 'what's up?'

'Go down the dump,' he mumbles.

'School, tomorrow.'

'Go after.' He smiles kind of twistedly. 'See the old man there. Stay a while. He'll give you something from me . . .'

Derek Gremlin Drives

Cuthbert Custardstain's the worst. The worst time's after school, when the bus drivers wait in their buses. Usually, once he's had a fag, he'll open the doors to let us in. The bus'll reek pretty badly all the way home, but Custardstain'll enjoy that. He's the kind of bus driver who thinks school buses would be fine without any school kids. I've got news for Custardstain. It isn't going to happen.

The name's Sean Piper, by the way. The BN 40 – that's our school bus – the BN 40 posse's the best and coolest there is. Custardstain doesn't think so. Most of the time, he makes life pretty evil. No opening windows.

No kneeling up on seats. No more than two to a seat. No eating. No wrappers. No music. Do not stand in the aisle. And especially, do not chew gum and stick it under the seats.

'Ladies first.' Custardstain said, when we went to get off the other day. Can you believe it, he made us wait till *every single girl* had got off? I wouldn't mind but he did it just to annoy us. That was the only reason. He's just as evil with the girls. He doesn't care about *ladies first* at all.

You'll have guessed by now, I hate him. It's really not hard to hate Custardstain. It's not just the reek and the hump on the back of his shoulder. It's the way he goes mad if you argue. It doesn't matter what you say, Custardstain always wins. It's easy to win when you're the driver. Big Man Custardstain gets a kick out of shouting at first years – he can be *really* sarcastic – so that they're practically wetting themselves when they finally get off the bus. He should take on someone his own size some time. Then he'd know what it felt like.

Probably the only other person I hate as much as Custardstain is Mr Fleiss. Mr Fleiss – his name means hard-working, which is always, yawn, the first thing he tells you when you start German in the first year (hard-working's the name, and I expect no less from *you*, *7G*) – Mr Fleiss has a thing about shirts. School shirts have to be tucked in *at all times*, even when you've come from PE. School ties have to be kipper-side-out when Fleiss is on the prowl, plus shirts tucked in so they look really dorky even when he isn't, in case he comes round the corner and goes off his face, which is something he does quite often. Three times untucked and it's a detention. Some people. He should take a ride with Custardstain. They could give each other a really hard time and save everyone else the bother.

As you know by now Custardstain's not the *best*-loved person we ever met, you won't be too surprised when I tell you no one wept when he ricked his back. Most people hoped it was terminal. The BN 40 posse hung out the towels. We hung 'em out of the school bus windows all the way home after swimming because Custardstain couldn't tell us not to. He'd have gone ballistic if he'd seen us. He *did* go ballistic when he saw us. It was worth driving the long way round, past his house. Nothing to worry about, Derek said. It wasn't as if Cuthbert had stitches or anything else he could rupture. Derek said jumping up and down with rage couldn't do Cuthbert's back much harm. It might even do it some good. Derek said quite a lot about Custardstain, right after we told him what Custardstain was like. But I haven't got on to that yet.

What I *have* got on to is Derek Gremlin. He told us that was his name. As relief driver, he'd be taking over the BN 40 route until Custardstain recovered or died, whichever happened soonest. It was funny, the way he arrived. He just turned up, one day, in the BN 40 after school, waiting in Cuthbert Custardstain's seat in the smoke-filled pit behind the wheel. As soon as he saw us coming, he jumped up and opened the door. 'Welcome aboard the BN 40.' He actually smiled. 'Your driver today is Derek Gremlin.'

It wasn't the wittiest thing anyone ever said, but he didn't say it nastily, the way Custardstain would have said it. He said it for real, with his eyes. *'Your driver today is Derek Gremlin.'*

'You mean,' I said, and it seemed like a dream, 'you mean Custardstain – Mr Cussons – isn't coming back?'

'Not for the moment, at least. I'm afraid he's hurt his back.' Derek Gremlin smiled. 'I hope you won't mind a new driver?'

'Whey-hey! Hang out the towels!' someone said – maybe Tom Lukes from 8H. 'Hear that? Custardstain broke his back! *He isn't coming back again, ever!'*

There was something about Derek Gremlin that made you like him right away. Maybe it was the way he asked everyone where they got off, well before each stop, instead of refusing to stop some places the way Custardstain did if he felt like it. Maybe it was the way he sang along with the radio as he drove, making faces like he *knew* how rubbish his singing was really, but didn't care who knew it. Maybe it was his laugh or his stupid fireman jokes. I don't know what it was that made you like him, but in no time we'd spilled our guts and told him *everything* about Cuthbert Custardstain. Derek's face darkened when he heard:

'– and one day, when Caroline Rapson wanted the stop *before* the stop she usually gets off at –'

'– because of going back to Isla Pierce's –'

'– well, Custardstain – Mr Cussons, I mean – Mr Cussons, he wouldn't stop for her –'

'– and she only had to walk up Gates Hill on her own, and her mum never wanted her to –'

'– plus, when she said it was a proper school stop –'

'– and he had no *right* not to let her off –'

'– he made her cry and told her he'd report her for insolence –'

Derek Gremlin Drives

Derek Gremlin's face grew dark as thunder, the more people moaned about Custardstain. After a while he stopped singing and did up his lips. It didn't take a genius to see old Cuthbert wasn't exactly Mr Popularity Plus. I suppose it surprised us all to find out how glad we were to get shot of him. The towels waving out of the windows seemed to say it all, *Happy sick leave, Cuthbert. Hope you never get better. No good wishes from your BN 40 Posse.*

'And one day, he told Miss Cravitz we cut up the seats –'

'– when no one even *touched* 'em –'

'– *and* he pushed Jeremy Steed off a seat, when it was the backseat –'

'– and sometimes he, like, lurches the bus *deliberately* when you stand up to get off at school –'

'– and then he goes, "You never learn, do you?" when everyone falls over.'

Suddenly Derek Gremlin snapped off the radio. Turning left at the out-of-town Tesco, he pulled up Boar's Hill and out onto the Hinch Park to Hexworthy road. Cussons – Custardstain lived out on the Hinch Park road, I knew.

Somewhere on Hinch Park Crescent.

'Where are we going?' someone asked.

'Old Cussons lives out this way somewhere. Down Hinch Park somewhere, isn't it?'

'Do you know Mr Cussons lives out this way?' I asked Derek Gremlin.

'As it happens, I do.' Derek swung the wheel round. 'Let's go home past his house,'

Derek drove us *way* out of our road and out onto the Hinch Park Estate. In no time we'd reached Custardstain's house. We gave it the slow drive-past, beeping as we went, so all the neighbours came out, Custardstain included. It was a real pleasure to see his reaction. He stood in the street and looked after us. You could practically see his jaw hitting the pavement, he opened his mouth so wide. Derek did impressions all the way home. We laughed – I'm not kidding – till we couldn't laugh any more. What a blast. What a day. What a driver.

Hanging out the towels that day was a good way to put up our Vs. I don't think anyone got over it for a week. Derek Gremlin hadn't planned it. He'd just got mad, and it had happened. Now I've told it, I can hardly believe it myself. But that was how School Bus BN 40 from Boundary Road Community College to Hexworthy

Derek Gremlin Drives

via Pagett's Cross came to do a drive-past through Hinch Park Crescent, swimming towels streaming, most people screaming, '*Cuthbert, eat our dust! We just called to say we love you – not!*'

Probably Custardstain got over it pretty quickly, once he'd finished dancing in the street. Probably he went in and kicked the dog or chewed out *Mrs* Custardstain. I didn't want to think about it. The best of it was, *we* never got chewed out for doing it. No one at home even knew what had happened until we told 'em. Derek was such a neat driver, we weren't even late getting in.

It was a brilliant start, and we never looked back with Derek Gremlin. Derek always had a joke. He was always ready to listen, and laugh at the goss. We even told him the Fleiss jokes. There were loads of jokes about Fleiss. Derek told some pretty good jokes himself, plus he didn't mind – within reason – what you did on the bus, so long as nothing got damaged and no one else minded, either. He never stopped us doing anything for *no good reason*, the way most school-bus drivers did. It was our school bus, Derek said. We should travel the way we wanted. Derek was cool. He was also the best – and safest – driver I've ever seen. Plus, he liked school kids. *Respect.*

Brainstorms

A week or two after the drive-past in Hinch Park Crescent – most people had heard about it by that time, and Derek was some kind of hero – Limner was sniffling on the back seat, the way he does all the time. Derek noticed it right away. Instead of starting up the BN 40, he got up and went to the back of the bus and started up a counselling session with Limner.

'Simon, isn't it? What's up with you?'

Dale Blixen piped up, 'It's Fleiss.'

'Fleiss?' Derek looked up. 'Would that be the stuffed shirt on bus duty?'

We all looked at Fleiss, busy hassling first years in the bus queues outside the library. You could practically hear the lecture he was dishing out through the – fantastically clean, since Derek – BN 40 windows. You, boy. Where's your bus-pass? I– I don't have it, sir. You don't have it. What does that make you? I'm sorry, sir, I don't know. I-said-what-does-that-make-you? (Hopelessly) Stupid, sir? No, it makes you *miss the bus*. Up to Reception for a temporary pass. Let's see those feet move. *Go*.

'Never mind him,' Derek said. 'You meet that sort all the time.'

Simon Limner nodded miserably. He was always getting picked on. 'Mr Fleiss goes, Limner, are those black trousers? I go, they're *blue-black*, sir. He goes, you know the rules. Navy trousers only. Detention.'

That evening on the way home, Derek Gremlin took us travelling. The way Derek took us travelling was through the way he made us see things. He'd been, Derek told us, all around Europe and everywhere because before he'd been a school-bus driver, he'd driven tour buses for Sky Holidays. That had been his job. He'd also done all the tour-guide stuff so he knew how to talk up a view. He talked up the view so well, all the way home that day, he made you believe you *saw* it. First, we went through France via Toulouse and the wine-growing Languedoc (Boundary Lane Estate through Slimeford Pike), then we crossed the Pyrenees (Handiford Down and Brew Tor), coming down over the plains of the Sierra Nevada (Pagett's Cross through Hexworthy) to finish up at the depot.

There was only me and Wellsy – Nathan Wells – left, after everyone else had got off. Usually I get off at the stop before the bus depot, like almost everyone else, but today it was worth the walk to ride to the depot with Derek. Ours was the last bus in. Derek parked it carefully. I wondered how long Derek would stay. I hoped the Custardstain back was bad. I'm sorry, but the battered old BN 40 would've look pretty sad, now, being driven by anyone else.

Derek killed the engine. 'That's it,' he said, 'ladees and genelmen, the end of your tour for today.'

Wellsy said, 'What about *your* house?'

'Yeah,' I said, 'we want to drive round past your house.'

'I don't have a house,' Derek said.

'You don't have a house? Why not?'

'Because I don't live anywhere.'

'Everyone's got to live *somewhere*.'

'Where do you sleep?' Wellsy asked.

'Where'd you think? On the bus.'

'On the bus? Are you serious?'

'It isn't that bad.' Derek winked. 'There's a lot you don't know about me.'

He wasn't wrong. There was plenty we didn't know. Like where did he come from, for starters. Derek was kind of mysterious. Once or twice – it isn't easy to say this – I caught a change in his face in the driver's mirror. Once or twice, just for a moment, Derek Gremlin's face looked like it would melt into just about *anything you wanted*, like – like he only gave *you* what *you* gave *him*, back. It made me feel strange. Was Derek Gremlin just

Derek Gremlin Drives

a driver? Or your own best wish for yourself? You want the best and coolest school-bus driver in the world? Dream you deserve him – you got it. Sometimes – and this is the weirdest – sometimes, just now and again if you watched him really closely, Derek Gremlin's head looked like it had a glow around it or something. Wellsy said we should see if he had a shadow, because things like ghosts and vampires never cast a shadow but – weirder still – the sun never seemed to come out wherever Derek was standing.

There were quite a few things – little things – you couldn't help noticing about Derek, like the way no one ever saw him eat. Custardstain used to eat all the time, mainly pork pies or Yorkies, or sometimes egg custards which stank after he dropped them all down himself while he was driving, one reason the Custardstain tag had stuck with him so long. But Derek was too cool to eat. Too cool to be our school-bus driver, even though Derek was a name that really hummed. Del's not bad, said Wellsy. Why don't we call you Del? But Derek Gremlin only laughed. He didn't mind what we called him. Whatever we called him, he'd still be Derek Gremlin. Where had he come from, anyway? I really wanted to know. Had he always been this way, or did he *learn* to be Derek Gremlin? If he did, where did he learn it – the College of Cool Bus Operatives? Did he pop out of some Gremlin factory or something? Hatch from a giant green egg? Or did he drop down, to make you think drivers were human, from the Great Bus Depot in the Sky? I wanted to ask him, but I couldn't. He had a way of stopping questions before they started. The most we were ever going to learn about Derek Gremlin we learnt on the day Derek kidnapped Fleiss. The kidnap started simply, with Fleiss and Sammy Saunders.

It was the end of the bus queue after school.

Everyone had got on the bus but Sammy Saunders. The BN 40 was late that day already. Derek had looked a bit grim. He'd folded away a letter – I'd forgotten about that letter – he'd folded away a letter just as we all got on, and he never had his usual joke or smile, the way he normally did. It was obvious something was up, looking back, but we never thought to ask him.

Instead, we watched Fleiss dump on Sammy.

'Late already.'

Sammy looked at Fleiss and said, 'Mr Fleiss, can you sign my note? So I can go home with Abel Speake?'

Fleiss looked at Sammy a moment. Then he said, 'Saunders, your tie is undone.'

Derek Gremlin Drives

They were standing, at the time, right beside the open BN 40 bus door. Me and Abel Speake were waiting just inside. Derek was waiting, too, frowning and listening and tapping both hands on the wheel. He'd started up the engine, and the good old BN 40 was juddering pretty nicely, the way it usually does before Derek knocks it in gear. All we had to do was get Fleiss to sign Sammy's permission note and get Damon Napely out of Sammy's seat – which Abel Speake had bagged already – go to first gear, let up the clutch, and we were away. But Fleiss had that look – I could tell it a mile off – the look that said, *Not in my ljfetime.*

'Mr Fleiss?' Quickly Sammy fixed his tie, then held up his note again to Fleiss. 'Mr Fleiss? Can you sign my permission note? Please?'

Fleiss took the note like it smelled. It had been written and signed by Sammy Saunders's mother to say that he had her permission to go home on the BN 40 with Abel Speake, the way the Head of Lower School insisted your parents write it if you got on *any school bus but the bus you were allocated to*. Fleiss knew the rules off by heart. I expect he made them up. He read Sammy Saunders's note slowly, looking him up and down as he read it, like he might find something *else* he could bug him about.

'So,' Fleiss said, 'your mother wrote this?'

'Yes, Mr Fleiss.' Sammy Saunders looked worried.

Derek revved the engine. He was tapping like mad on the wheel. I knew that tap. I knew how he felt, I really did. It was the kind of tap that builds slowly before something drastic.

'Let me see, now –' Fleiss cleared his throat and held up the note. For some reason, no one'll ever know why, he decided to read it aloud,

'"Dear" – spelled D-e-e-r – "Deer Head of Lowr" – the e's left out – "Deer Head of Lowr School, I give my pemissno" – that's p-e-m-i-s-s-n-o – "for Samuel to og to Abel Speake's,"' Mr Fleiss smiled nastily: 'I take it you want to *og* to Abel Speake's?' He went on before Sammy could say anything, '"Please coud Samuel go no BN 40? Yours sinercly, A.N. Saunders."'

'Well?' He looked at Sammy. 'Go no BN 40?'

'She means go *on* the BN 40,' Sammy said. 'She gets her letters mixed up.'

'She does, does she? Would that be before or *after* she learned to spell like you?'

Derek Gremlin Drives

By this time Sammy was bright red. He blinked a lot when he said, 'I'm sorry, my mum's dyslexic.'

'You're asking me to believe an *adult* wrote this note?' Fleiss was out of control. He hadn't even heard what Sammy'd said. 'Here's a tip – if you're going to fake a permission note, *either get the spelling right or make it even worse*. Then we'll know you wrote it straightaway.'

Derek tapped hard, then harder. It was hard to believe what Fleiss had done. Harder for Sammy to say it. 'Dyslexia makes you spell things wrong. My mum gets words muddled up. She can't help it. No one knew she was dyslexic all the time she was at school.'

'In that case –'

'That's why the note looks funny. She doesn't like writing notes. Sometimes I write them for her, only it looks like I made them up.'

'That,' said Fleiss, 'is exactly how it looks.'

'I wouldn't make this up, Mr Fleiss.' Sammy's voice had gone really quiet. 'I wish she could write things better. She's really clever, my mum.'

The tapping from Derek suddenly stopped. Most people knew Sammy sometimes wrote notes for his mother but no one was too bothered why. Now everyone *knew* why, and Fleiss had made Sammy say it. No one had ever heard Fleiss apologize for anything, ever, in his life. Everyone waited. *Say* it.

But instead of saying sorry, Fleiss ripped up the note slowly.

'I don't like deception, Saunders. I think we both know who wrote this note. *And* who's ringing your mother.'

'Right,' someone said. '*That's it.*'

And Derek Gremlin kind of *exploded* out of his cab into Harald Fleiss. Next thing, old Fleiss was inside the bus with Sammy Saunders, the doors snapped shut, and we were off and out of the school gates and down the road at speed, the good old BN 40 pumping up through her gears like she was a GT racing bus or something.

'Sit down, Mr Fleiss,' Derek warned. 'No Standing in the Aisles while the Vehicle is in Motion.'

'I'm sorry – why am I here?'

'Thought you'd appreciate a lift.' Derek Gremlin smiled, and something passed between him and Harald Fleiss. Maybe it was a look in the eye, maybe it was the Gremlin 'fluence, maybe it was a guilty conscience – who knows what made Fleiss sit down? But he sat down by Sammy, pretty quiet, and he stayed pretty quiet all the way out on the bypass till Slimeford Approaches, when he suddenly got quite excited. It seemed we were passing his house. He even bobbed up in his seat, to see over Damon Napely.

'No kneeling up on the seats,' Derek Gremlin said, calmly.

'I'm sorry?'

'You'd better sit down, Mr Fleiss,' Derek's eyes, reflected in his mirror, bored right through Harald Fleiss. 'Or we'll make you sit in the toilet.'

Everyone laughed. The toilet at the back of the bus made the whole bus stink. The thought of Fleiss trapped inside it was majorly funny. As funny as it was, it was well over the top. Kidnapping Fleiss on the school bus home. Threatening Fleiss with the toilet, even as a joke. I looked at Wellsy, and Wellsy looked at me. Wouldn't he get the sack? How did Derek *dare*?

Mr Fleiss sat down. 'Please,' he said. 'I want –'

'No registered stops until Pagett's Cross.' Derek said, smooth as silk.

'But I need to get off before Slimeford.'

'No stopping, unless at registered stops.'

'Well, yes, in *theory*,' Fleiss said, red in the face. 'In *theory*, no stopping, I suppose, but –'

'Can't compromise bus safety, I'm afraid.' Derek threw Fleiss a look to melt his dentures. 'It's a matter of risk insurance. I have to drive by the rule.'

'Risk insurance, of course, of course.' Fleiss nodded like a madman, glad to agree, for some reason, with anything Derek Gremlin said. 'Of course, I understand.' He was always on about insurance himself. No diving into the pool. No staying late in the gym. No unsupervised visits anywhere, at any time. *We're not insured for it* seemed like a good reason not to do anything. Probably you shouldn't even get up in the morning, if you weren't insured for it.

It was an unreal kind of journey especially for Sammy Saunders. He bumped along next to Harald Fleiss, they soon got talking about cricket – Fleiss is huge on cricket – and finally both of them were gassing so much they never even noticed we'd pulled out and away across the moor. It was one of Derek's Magical Mystery Tours. The Mystery was, how no one was ever late home. The Magic was, all the things that we saw.

Lately things'd got weirder than the tour-guide stuff Derek gave us earlier. *Deep* travel, Derek called it. After we'd been driving a while, something'd sort of *click over* inside the bus, so that time went by ever-so-slowly, and the things that rushed by outside looked kind of milky somehow, as though they were standing in glue. Sometimes we saw things we never should've seen out of *any* school-bus window, things like mountains and valleys and rivers, mines and jewels and waterfalls, bullocks and carts and paddy-fields, maharajahs and kings. Once we even passed an entire Roman army, another time it was a plane crash. Derek said, 'That's Buddy Holly, that is, lying dead in the snow.' I can't describe how it made me feel. Mainly sad, I suppose.

We often went a funny way round on the way home. Probably the BN 40 route looked like a spider-trail over the map, we went so many different ways. No one ever worked out how we went so far, but *still* made the depot on time. That was the mysterious part. You never knew where they'd take you – that was Derek's tours. Tonight it was Brew Tor and the Midgeons. The Midgeons was this giant stack of boulders on top of Brew Tor. Under Brew Tor was a car park, often – like today – with a Willa's Ices van parked in it. It wasn't the first time we'd stopped there. How was I to know it would be the last?

Derek pulled in with his usual smile. But when he got up, his face was sad already. 'I hope you enjoyed your trip today – all your trips – with me. I hope we've had fun together.' Derek paused and swallowed. 'The reason I've brought you up here today is,' he held up the letter I'd seen him with earlier, 'I've brought you all here today to read you this letter. I've got good news and bad news. Which d'you want first?'

It all seemed kind of solemn, the way Derek said it. A hum and a whisper ran round the bus.

No one wanted the bad news at all. Even Fleiss shook his head.

'Bad news!' Limner shouted suddenly, like the idiot that he was. '*No! Not bad!*' Everyone else slammed him down. '*We want good news first!*' Limner made a face. 'Well. I thought it would get it over with.'

'The good news,' Derek smiled, 'the good news is, that Mr Cussons *isn't coming back.*'

Everyone cheered and drummed their feet so long that finally Derek held up his hand for us to stop. 'Mr Cussons is retiring, due to ill health,' Derek grinned, 'so I know you'll want to wish him all the best –'

'All the best lumps in his custard pies!' someone shouted.

'The best hospital for his ugly mug!'

'The best psychiatrist!'

Derek Gremlin Drives

'Neck-brace!'

'Strait-jacket!'

'Which brings me to the bad news,' Derek held up his letter for silence. 'This is from my boss at Raleigh Transport,' He cleared his throat and read: '"Dear Mr Gremlin, I am writing to inform you that from Monday 7th March, Mr Bernard Reynolds has been appointed to the permanent position of Driver for School-bus Contract 8839. Your contract with Raleigh Transport is therefore terminated forthwith."' He looked around the bus. 'Forthwith means today. This is our last drive together. I know you'll welcome Bernard Reynolds, your new driver, on Monday. You've been the best. But this is goodbye from Derek Gremlin.'

Derek sat down suddenly. Everyone seemed kind of stunned.

'I'm sorry?' said Harald Fleiss. 'Is there some way they can terminate your contract so suddenly?'

'We've made some pretty wild detours,' Derek said, sadly. 'I think I terminated myself.'

'But we don't *want* anyone else driving the BN 40.' I jumped up. 'Do we? Not Cussons, not Bernard Reynolds, not *anyone* but Derek, right? Gremlin *in*, Gremlin *in* –'

They all started up, 'Gremlin *in*, Gremlin *in*, Gremlin –'

'It's nice of you,' Derek looked misty, 'more than nice, but what's done's done. And I'm glad we did it, aren't you?'

'Der-*ek*, ma-*gic*, Der-*ek*, ma-*gic* –' The BN 40 posse let him *know* we were. But there was nothing we could do. The empty space he was going to leave had started to open up already. Derek Gremlin, why couldn't you stay? Did it *have* to end? Was it really too good to be true?

'You're good with these kids, you really are,' Fleiss watched us raise the roof. 'How on earth d'you do it?'

Derek Gremlin smiled, a long, slow smile that threw back everything, with interest, we were throwing at *him*. 'It isn't hard, they're great.'

'What will you do now?' Wellsy asked, really quietly, after Fleiss took the first years for Tangle Twisters from Willa's Ices outside.

'What else would I do? Drive, of course,' Derek Gremlin winked. 'I don't know anything else.'

But I think he did. I think Derek Gremlin knew a whole lot more than he was letting on. How come I saw him on telly a week later, *driving a stretch limo on*

Derek Gremlin Drives

Newsnight, if he didn't? I practically jumped out of my seat when I saw him. 'Dad!' I said, 'Look! It's our school-bus driver, Derek Gremlin!'

'Don't be daft.' Dad nearly choked on his cottage pie when I nudged him. 'Don't be daft,' he said, 'one of your school-bus drivers driving a head of state to a world conference? Not very likely, is it?'

About as *likely*, I was going to say, as a mystery tour through a rajah's palace or dreamy fields of wheat. About as likely as Mr Fleiss's turnaround into someone much nicer than he had been. About as likely as any one of a dozen things that Derek Gremlin did.

That's what I was *going* to say. But in the end, I didn't.

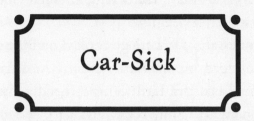

Car-Sick

Ever been really car-sick? Pale as paper? Hating the *smell* of cars? With parents that just don't get it, like mine?

My olds don't *understand* about car-sickness. They don't know what it's like to be just-about-all right until the car tilts a certain way or the heater's up too much or the plastic smell of the seats just tips you over the edge. They sit merrily upfront arguing or whatever else they do, and they don't understand at all. Have *they* ever felt like hurling every time the car takes a bridge or a hairpin, a bump or even a *traffic light?*

Excuse me if! I feel quite strongly about this, but I *do* suffer most weekends. Most weekends I spend hours in the car with my parents with my stomach swilling around like a milk factory, and then there's the embarrassment, when Dad gets road rage on wheels. 'Let's go out,' he says. 'Let's go for a run in the country.' He drives, like, *all afternoon* through villages called Piddle Henbottom or Little Stuffit, then finally he stops at a pub with no family room and it's Coke and crisps in the car for yours truly, thank *you* very much. Cars. I tell you, I'm *sick* of 'em.

The Tantra's not a bad car. Your Tantra represents an ideal synthesis of advanced technology, outstanding safety, environmental compatibility and economy in operation, the Owner's Manual says. I have plenty of time to read the Owner's Manual when I'm stuck in the car outside a pub. The Tantra offers technical sophistication and exceptional comfort. It's just that I'm sick of it. We go out motoring – that's what the olds call it, motoring – we go out motoring most weekends, mainly to garden centres and stately homes, steam rallies, fêtes, you name it. My olds're a lot older than most people's. I don't think they meant to have me. I think I was quite a surprise.

The joys of motoring, they say. Apart from the odd cream tea and a bag of crisps at a pub, I'd like to know what they *are*. I said to 'em, 'Let *me* drive. You sit there, heartless parents. See what it feels like, endlessly going somewhere you don't know, feeling sick, with no idea when feeling sick will *ever end*, when you never wanted to come out *anyway*. Oh, and throw in dying of embarrassment and fear every time your driver – that's me – throws a wobbly in a car park or on a one-way system in some fume-filled, gridlocked town centre.'

I'm kidding, of course. I never said, 'Let me drive.' But I've felt like it plenty of times. Especially the day we had one of Dad's little runs in the country – I thought we'd *never* get there – about eighty miles plus wrong turnings and wild-goose chases (we do a lot of those) to Bullimore Wildlife Park. So we're going along, and Dad says to Mum, 'Where's the map?'

'Map?' Mum says. 'What map?'

'Are we nearly there?' I say. 'I'm feeling really sick.'

'The map,' Dad says, 'of West Dorset.'

'South and East Wiltshire,' Mum says, 'Hampshire, Somerset . . .' She surfaces from the car pocket with Devon and South East Cornwall. 'No West Dorset here, I'm afraid.'

'I'm sick,' I say. 'Can't we stop?'

Car-Sick

'I thought you'd got Robert some pills,' Dad says.

'I did,' Mum says. 'Robert, have you taken those pills?'

'Yes.' I lie. 'I took two.'

'Well, then, you'll be just fine.'

'Right,' I say, 'you'd know.'

Let me tell you about travel-sickness pills. Travel-sickness pills are like torches and glue – they don't work. My mate Christow went up to London on the coach not so long ago. He goes, 'I got my travel sickness pills. I took two before I got on.' Know what he goes and does? My mate Steve Christow only goes and downs a whole bag of Flumps and takes a seat over the heaters. Then he's surprised he chucks up halfway. So much for travel-sickness pills. They came up whole, Christow says. They hadn't even dissolved.

So I don't take pills, I put up with it. Some people say you grow out of travel-sickness. 'Don't worry,' they say, 'you'll grow out of it.' The way you grow out of curly hair or sticking-out ears, I suppose. Some people say it's all in your mind. The power of suggestion, etc. I'd like to suggest to *them* they sit in the back of our car on a winding country road, in summer, with the windows done up because Dad won't have them down.

The car vents, you see, are an adequate draught for anyone. Except someone with their guts in their mouth.

I'm sorry, but that's how it feels. Especially when Dad never stops.

Usually we go on and on, because Dad can't decide where to pull in, or he doesn't *want* to pull in until he finds the ultimate pit-stop, so he goes on and on and *on,* past pubs offering grub, family rooms, warmth, puppies, discos, their fortune, a bank account and villa in *Spain* if you'll only pull in, except that Dad won't, until even *Mum* feels faint and begs him to stop.

Sometimes a toilet break works. 'I need a toilet,' I say. 'I have to have one now.' It's usually good for a five-minute stop in a field or a breath of fresh air at some petrol station where Dad stocks up on wine gums and soft drinks so he can keep going on for *ever.* They can't ignore the toilet call, the way they can car-sickness – I've only ever actually chucked up once in the car, and that was when I was three, so naturally it's all in my mind and I'm making it up – so toilet stops are one way to make Dad pull in when I get really desperate. Except once it backfired badly.

The only reason I'm even *mentioning* the Exit

Car-Sick

Seventeen Episode, is to show you how bad it gets. We're on the motorway, right, when I want to go, like, *badly.* Dad says, 'Hang on, Robert.'

Services twenty miles. Then what happens? He only 'forgets' and misses the Branscombe Services exit – exit sixteen, that is my last chance for forty-seven miles. Well, I don't think I need to spell it out. I think you can see what's coming. After I'd filled up our sandwich box behind the car off exit seventeen with half of southern England speeding past, I felt like I'd hit rock bottom. Whatever the filling in the Terminal Sandwich of Motorway Shame was, I'd eaten it with mayo. And all because Dad couldn't stop.

So we're going along to Bullimore, and: 'Are you all right, Robert?' Mum goes.

'No,' I say, 'I'm dying.'

'Won't be long now. Almost there.'

They always say that. It's supposed to make you feel better.

'You can't go wrong if you look straight ahead.' Dad checks me in his mirror. 'Eyes on the horizon, that's the way.'

'Pull yourself together. Eyes on the horizon.' They always say that, as well. Let me deal with this one.

Keeping your eyes on the horizon when you feel like *visiting* the horizon with half your stomach contents is about as much help as stoking a fire just before it burns the house down. Plus *you* try seeing past Dad's head when he's just got his jaws around half a pound of wine gums. The horizon isn't even in sight.

The day we visit Bullimore I sit in the front halfway, which is all right except for Dad's driving. I decide I'd rather be car-sick than tongue-lashed by Dad for map-reading a nanosecond too slowly – reading the map turns my stomach over, anyway – or suggesting we go by any way other than the Official Dad-approved Route. I actually ask him to stop so I can crawl back to my accustomed place of torture, the back seat. You can get used to anything after a while.

So we motor *for ever* and we finally get to Bullimore Wildlife Park about eleven forty-five in the morning, by which time I'm feeling so grisly I just don't *care* any more. I'm thinking they can wrap me up in a car rug and just about go on for *ever* – Chile, Uruguay, Java, what do *I* care? – when Dad knocks a hole in the car park. This is after we drive in at the wrong entrance and a ranger with a mobile phone makes us drive out again, which makes Dad mad to start with. Then what happens is, he reverses and doesn't see the post. Of course, right away it's the post's fault.

'What the *devil* –?'

'Clive,' Mum says, 'we've hit a post.'

'I can see that,' Dad says. 'I'm not stupid. What the hell is it *doing* there?'

He jams the car into first gear and shoots forward, then into reverse and goes back, then forward again, then back, swearing a lot in between. Pretty soon, people are staring. After two hours in the car I already feel like the last crisp in the packet. Now I feel like crying, but I don't.

At last Dad stops the car. Christow and me get out. I didn't mention before we had Christow with us. My parents never understand why I want a mate along. 'It's nice,' they say, 'just the three of us. Why do you want Steven Christow?' Why do they *think* I want someone my own age along? I can't exactly say 'So I can have some *fun*. To break the tension, you know?' Mum, Dad, me, me, Mum, Dad. Just the three of us. It's so intense sometimes. They wouldn't understand if I told them. My parents are just so *old,* you know? They don't understand a thing.

So after we hit the post in the car park at Bullimore

Wildlife Park, Christow helps me out of the car. After chucking up Flumps on the London Rapide, he understands how I'm feeling.

I don't actually dry-heave in the bushes, but for a while I come close. After my mouth stops watering I just feel sort of light-headed, like I'm here but it's not really me. That's how I normally feel when we arrive anywhere in the car. Usually I'm just beginning to feel all right again when I have to get back in to go back home. But not this time. This time we have to examine the car in detail, once Dad finally has it parked. I have plenty of time to sit down and get over motion-sickness. Motion-sickness has nothing on embarrassment once Dad gets out of his pram. He gets out and kicks the post. 'Ruddy thing,' he says. 'They want their bumps felt,' he says. 'Putting ruddy posts in, just under the line of people's vision.'

For once, I'm feeling OK. The Tantra's OK, too, once Dad can actually see it through the red mist of rage over his eyes. Damage is minimal, considering. Only a bash on the bumper. A knocked-over wooden post. And most people thinking we're mad.

'Could be worse,' Christow jokes. 'Could've been concrete or something.'

Car-Sick

'That's right,' Dad says. 'We're lucky to get into the car park so lightly. We ought to be grateful they haven't mined it or put up rolls of barbed wire.'

'Now, Clive,' Mum says, 'take the chairs out.'

'We shan't want the chairs until later.'

'I'm only meaning,' Mum says, 'take out the chairs from under the picnic. Did I not tell you that flask's got to be right side up?'

'Not in the last five minutes, you didn't,' Dad says. 'I don't think I heard Mum say Right Side Up in the last five minutes, did you, Steven?'

Christow doesn't understand Dad's sense of humour. *I* don't understand Dad's sense of humour. Plus he actually calls Mum, *Mum,* as in: 'Have you packed the salt and pepper, Mum?' or: 'Ask Mum if she's heard.' It isn't so bad when it's just the three of us – I've kind of got used to it, you know? But with friends around Dad's a nightmare, he really is. It's actually so bad I had to try to ask him not to do it. 'I've got Christow coming,' I said. 'Can you not call Mum "Mum"?'

'What?' Dad said. 'I like that. I'll call Mum anything I like.'

So just because I ask him not to, he calls Mum 'Mum' even more. He really overdoes it in the Grazing

Animals and Elephants Compound. Mum's never been so be-Mummed.

'Would that be a baby giraffe, Mum, what do you think?'

'Looks like it, doesn't it?' Mum says.

'Antelope in far west of compound, it says here. Elephants to your right. Approach All Animals with Caution. Drive-Through Predator and Monkey Park – we'll probably do that after lunch. Then there's Hippo Lake. What about it, Mum? Shall we do that after lunch?'

'What are you asking *me* for?' Mum says. 'Would you boys like to go off on your own, and we'll all meet up again later?'

Later is one o'clock for warmish egg-and-salad-cream sandwiches and even warmer lemonade – I hate lemonade, what makes anyone *like* it? – after, Christow and I at least get to see the elephants without Dad asking Mum what she thinks of them. Christow and I think they're smart. Especially the baby elephants. They rush up to the fence as soon as they see us and feel us all over with their trunks. I never realized baby elephants have wiry black bristles sticking out all over their backs, but they do. You should go to Bullimore and feel 'em.

Car-Sick

Dad makes Christow sit on an aluminium fold-out chair and balance a plastic plate on his knee to eat his lunch. I really want a picture of that. 'Dad, can I take a picture?' I jump up and hold out my hand. He hands me the camera after he's given me a million instructions for taking a snap with it, the way he always has to. I don't take it straightaway. First I leave my Swiss roll.

'Not eating much, Robert?' Dad says.

'I can't really, can I?' I say. 'Not if you don't want me being sick all over the back of the car on the way home.'

'Get something down you,' Dad barks. 'No wonder you look like a ghost.'

I back off so I get Bullimore House in the background, then – *snap*! I take the picture at the moment Dad's adjusting his trousers. Always good for a laugh.

I hate him, I tell the camera. *If I could make him sick, I would.*

'Go on, Dad, have mine,' I say, when I get back onto the car rug. 'I don't really like warm Swiss roll. You might as well finish it up.'

'Don't mind if I do,' Dad says, polishing off a Scotch egg.

'Have some more tea, as well.' Christow watches me tip in sugar. 'How about Hippo Lake after?'

'After what?' Dad asks, troughing down Swiss roll and sweet tea.

'After lunch, you said. Want my last sandwich, as well?'

Christow reads out the leaflet. '"Hippo Lake and Crocodile Alley. Waterproof Coats for Hire. Not for the faint-hearted", it says here. Can we do that next?'

'I think I might go for a walk,' Dad says. 'Which way did it say to the toilets?'

Dad wanders off to find the toilets. When he comes back he's actually been to the shop and brought himself a cold beer as well. His face shines. The sun beats down. 'It's hot,' he says. 'Chin, chin.'

After lunch we finally get out on to Hippo Lake after the olds try their best to get out of it. They try to make out they'd rather walk the Flamingo Trail and come back round by the rhinos. At least, that's what Dad makes out.

'Come on, Dad,' I say. 'The boat looks really good. Plus you can take some pictures.'

'I don't know,' Dad says doubtfully. 'I think Mum wants a walk – you want a walk, don't you, Mum?'

'I don't know what I want, really.' Mum's giving the White Water Ride the eye. 'It looks quite exciting,' she says.

Car-Sick

We join the queue anyway, arguing. Hippo Lake looks cool. Basically, there's this huge great lake with an island and boats go around it on a tour and hippos pop up – if you're lucky – and you take a picture of them, or you can buy a picture of them afterwards that looks like a snap you *might've* taken of them if they *don't* pop up, which they might not. Or you can buy a Combined Ticket for Crocodile Alley, and go down the White Water rapids as well, which is favourite with Christow and me.

'There's buffalo compounds two and three on the Flamingo Trail, it says here.' Dad whips out his brochure again. 'We could come back round by the rhinos.'

'I can't believe you still want to go on a *walk*.'

'I haven't lost the use of my legs yet, Robert.'

'Don't you fancy the boats, or what?'

'Not madly, no, I don't.'

'Come on, Dad, what's the difference?' He's not getting out of it that easily. '"White Water Thrills" it says here. You might as well go in a boat as walk around in this heat.'

I'm looking after Dad's interests. I'm cunning when I want to be, see?

'Robert's right,' Mum says. 'It's too hot to walk in this heat.'

'I don't really feel,' Dad says, 'like being trussed up in a plastic mac.'

'You can always get wet, if you want.' Christow's enjoying this, now.

'What's that?'

'Get some white water down you.' I say. 'No wonder you run into posts.'

'I'm not sure,' Dad says, looking vaguely like thunder, 'I'm not sure I *need* Hippo Lake.'

'Oh, come on, Clive,' Mum says, 'you really are an old woman.'

'Well, thanks very much,' Dad says. 'I don't *think*,' Dad says, 'I've done anything to deserve *that*.'

We reach the edge of the quay and use our Combined Tickets. Mum and Dad hire see-through plastic macs that do up under their chins and make them look like pre-packed instant dinners, and we climb into this daggy old tourist showboat with about twenty other people also done up in plastic, all except Christow and me and a few other kids who'd rather be wet than sad. Dad doesn't look too happy, but he's in.

So we get out on to Hippo Lake, and the first thing that happens is, we find out the wind's got up and it isn't as calm as it looks. The deck rolls a bit but Dad gets his feet under the seat in front of him and pulls out his camera and soon he's snapping away at completely blank stretches of water where hippos' ears might have been sighted at some distant time in the past. We circle Baboon Island with no baboons in sight. Then we get out the bait buckets and chuck bloody bits of fish over the side, but still no joy with the hippos, which are veggies anyway, as even Christow points out, but this doesn't stop all the olds on board snapping away with their cameras like maniacs, when suddenly *seals* pop up all around us, and they really are the business – I mean, they're great. They're really close, so you can see their big sad eyes and their whiskers and their funny, closed-in ears and the mottled marks on their skins. Christow and me bung them *loads* of fish. And then we're back at the jetty and into Crocodile Alley.

We change boats for Crocodile Alley. At this point, Dad looks upset. The sun's pretty fierce by now. Dad's plastic mac has completely steamed up. He looks like a jar of pickled eggs.

'What's the matter, Clive?' Mum says.

'Feel a bit squiffy actually.' Dad burps into his hand. 'I shouldn't have eaten cucumber. Cucumber never agrees with me.'

'It doesn't agree with beer and eggs,' Mum reminds him. 'I thought you were eating a lot,' Mum says, 'but I didn't say at the time.'

So we're all four of us sat in this bright blue inflatable, when it slides off down Crocodile Alley, Christow and me really up for it, Dad up for something else, probably.

'You think they'd give you a dry boat at least,' Dad complains. 'These seats are soaking wet and there's quite a lot of water in the –'

The first wave hits us in the face just as we're going round a bend. Christow and I hang on and shout like madmen. The next bend flings us straight down this funnel into a whirlpool, then along this canal with tanks of real crocs either side. They can't get at us, of course, but they're so close you can see they'd like to. We bang against both sides of the canal and spin round lots of times, then we get sucked down some rapids that throw Mum and Dad together, then throw them apart again. Dad isn't enjoying himself. He hangs on and looks really green.

'NOT LONG NOW!' I shout to Dad.

'WHAT?' Dad looks like death. 'I CAN'T HEAR A THING YOU'RE –'

'BRILLIANT, ISN'T IT?'

Dad doesn't think it's brilliant. He looks like he'll throw up his guts. Before I have a chance to feel sorry for him, a wave smashes me right in the face. *NOT FEELING SICK, ARE WE? HANG ON TIGHT AND SUFFER, YOU SELFISH, UNFEELING OLD BLIMP.* That's not what I shout, but I feel like it. He can't hear a thing in the rapids. I *could* shout anything I like.

'COME ON, DAD! STOP MAKING A FUSS ABOUT NOTHING!'

We go *down* a chute and *round* some kind of island and *over* a weir into a splash-pool, which rolls us round a bend and into some kind of tunnel – and *out* of the tunnel into daylight, and serious white water. Poor old Dad. He grips the side. I almost feel sorry for him this time.

'DOESN'T FEEL TOO GOOD, DOES IT?'

'Uh?'

'EYES ON THE HORIZON! PULL YOURSELF TOGETHER! COME ON – YOU'RE ALL RIGHT!'

'ROBERT! WHAT ARE YOU SHOUTING ABOUT?' Mum puts her hand over mine. She's doing well. Her eyes are bright. She's had the ride of her life. 'IS IT NEARLY OVER NOW?' she shouts.

Brainstorms

It *is* nearly over. So's Dad – nearly over the side. As we swirl into calmer waters and the high-pressure jets hit us, making sure we finish wet through if we're not completely soaked already, poor Dad's blowing chunks over the side of the boat, and the back of his neck's really red. No one looks back to see the trail we've made in the water, but I guess it features ham and eggs, Swiss roll and cucumber. Christow and I look at each other. Chucking up Flumps on the London Rapide has nothing on polluting the entire White Water Ride system at Bullimore Wildlife Park in front of a million people, thank *you* very much. Whatever the filling in the Terminal Sandwich of Theme Park Shame, Dad just ate it with flags on.

No one does anything much for quite a long time after that. Christow and me do stickers in the *Wildlife Wonders* book Mum scores in the shop, a bit childish really, but I like childish things sometimes. Mum packs up the boot. Dad lies down and groans. After he's had a good lie-down on the rug in the shade of the Tantra and Mum's finished packing away the picnic, we all climb back into the car.

No one says anything.

Then: 'What's next?' says Christow. 'That was brilliant.'

Car-Sick

Mum says, 'What was brilliant?'

'Hippo Lake.'

Dad groans.

'Plus Crocodile Alley was *cool*.'

The back of his neck's faintly green. Dad starts up the car.

'Not going yet, are we?' I ask. 'What about the Drive-Thru Predator & Monkey Park?' I ask. 'Aren't we going to drive through them?'

Dad puts the car into gear. 'I can do without monkeys,' he says.

The drive home's a big improvement on the drive out, I have to say. For one thing, Dad doesn't argue. He leaves Mum to navigate, and Mum gets on and navigates us to a pub where there's this cool family room with bar-billiards and video games and the sausage and chips is really good. Dad drinks mineral water quietly and doesn't say very much, but Christow and I play Defenders and Grand Prix and Spacehogs and I wipe Christow *out* at bar-billiards, but he takes it well because he's Christow.

Dad takes the motorway almost all the rest of the way home, and it's fast and straight, so I don't feel sick hardly at all. He doesn't bother with villages named

Whiddle Piddlington or Up Barfing or twisty roads or churches or anything. I can't tell him how much better it is, so I don't even try. I'm suddenly glad I didn't laugh at him, when he was throwing up off the boat. I felt like it, but I didn't. Because I know how it feels.

'Why can't we always go on the motorway?' I ask.

'It's not very picturesque,' Mum says.

'No,' I say, 'but it's straighter.'

'Good, wasn't it?' Christow says. 'The elephants, I mean. And the seals. I liked the seals, did you like the seals Mrs Rendell?'

'I liked Crocodile Alley,' Mum says. 'I thought it was really astounding.'

'Feeling all right, Robert?' Dad asks.

'Brilliant, thanks,' I say. 'Thanks for going a straight way home. It makes a lot of difference.'

'Pity about the monkeys,' Christow says.

'You don't want to bother with monkeys,' Dad says. 'Those monkeys,' Dad says, 'all they do is snap off your radio aerial and peel off your window trim. Bloke at work drove his Vectra through that monkey park and the monkeys pulled off his wipers. He left his window trim in the road. *And* his tow-bar cover.'

Dad checks me out in his rear-view mirror. I smile,

and Dad smiles back. He still looks pale, he still doesn't know how I'm feeling. Is it his fault he's old and he knows it? But somehow I have a feeling Dad just might be more sympathetic in future. He might choose straight roads more often. He might even open some windows. If I'm car-sick, he'll understand.

'Dad's right,' I say. 'Who *cares* about seeing monkeys? I'm *sick* of monkeys.' I say.

The Ghost of Christmas Shopping

I'm a ghost, right? Haunting's my job. I get up and around, most years, about December the twenty-third. Or maybe the twenty-fourth. Call me lazy but I never went much on getting up before I had to. There was a time, back when it's hard to remember, when I spent my *ljfe* in bed. In hospital, that was. Then I got so I was okay to go home. Then I could go out shopping, so long as I didn't overdo it, or carry anything heavy. I left carrying things to Mum. I had to be careful a lot. I'm careful now. Catch me getting out of the freezer much before December the twenty-third, and you've got an exceptionally fine Christmas shopping frenzy.

The Ghost of Christmas Shopping

I usually start flexing the old haunting muscles about the time most kids finally realize the chocolate in the advent calendar's the grisliest ever invented. Once the shoppers in the supermarket get that glazed look, when they'll buy just about *anything* with 'Festive Special' on it, that's about the time I stretch my legs. When they open up the freezer for those last-minute cocktail-size sausage rolls, that's my wake-up call. It's shopping fever that warms me up and sets me on my feet. Call me shallow, but I love that stuff. I suppose you could call me the ghost of Christmas shopping, except no one calls me anything. Ever. I did have another name, once.

Usually, I wake up in the frozen turkeys. Then I huff out when someone opens the freezer – you *can* have enough of frozen turkeys, know what I mean? Soon as I'm out of the freezer, I'm checking out trolleys for a likely family to hang out with over Christmas. A really classic trolley always grabs me.

So this year I'm cruising the aisles, right, and the trolleys are looking pretty mediocre, nothing too appealing when I *actually spot the Stantons*. I almost *die*, except I did that already. See, I almost made it to lunchtime, last Christmas Day, with the Stantons.

Except for Danny Stanton's puppy, I might be there now. The stuff with the puppy almost killed me all over again. *Look at him, isn't he great? What shall I call him? Rusty? Come on, Rusty. Thanks, Mum, thanks, Dad. I really, really love him.*

Phew. Too much of that stuff, and I'm gone. Back in the freezer till next year. Love, generosity, Christmas spirit – it really turns me off. Call me freezer-fungus, only don't give me any of that heartwarming stuff. Maybe I *am* freezer-fungus, but I have to have something to feed off, you know. Even mould needs something to work with. I have to have hurt feelings, or at least a bit of rage. But Christmas spirit gets me. It makes me throw, it really does. I have to go back to my freezer. I don't have a lot of choice. It was too much to hope I'd make it through with the Stantons. Far too selfless, the Stantons. Pretty bleak Christmas all round.

So I've never yet made a whole Christmas day with *anyone.* So I'm thinking this year could be a first, and I'm chilling out on the corner between the deli and the Country Baker Mince Pie Offer, when I spot the perfect trolley. Very low fruit content, triple-choc super-soft ice cream *plus* soft drinks so bright they bring on an additive high just *looking* at them. This is a trolley I can relate to.

The Ghost of Christmas Shopping

I tag along after the family. Mum, Dad, boy, girl. The little girl could be a problem. The little girl sees straight through me, and I know she's got me sussed.

'Kelly,' Mum asks her, 'wake up. What colour jelly d'you fancy?'

'Blackcurrant,' goes Kelly, staring hard. 'Tell him to go away.'

'Who?' says Mum. 'Lawrie?'

It looks like Lawrie's the brother. He's not much older than Kelly. He could be *younger* than Kelly, who knows? What am I, expert on children?

'Not *Lawrie*.' Old Kelly's going to blow it in a minute. I dredge up a smile, but she pulls Mum's coat and points. 'Not Lawrie' she says, '*that* boy. Why's he following us?'

Mum looks round. 'What boy? Lawrie, get me a cheesecake mix. Down a bit. Left a bit. There.'

'Go away!' Kelly pouts. 'I don't *like* that boy.'

Phew. I make a face. It doesn't matter what I do. Mum's not really listening.

'Push the trolley,' says Mum, 'good girl. Let's get some biscuits, shall we? How about one of those selection tins with the pink wafers in it, would you like that?'

Lawrie drops a packet of cheesecake mix into the trolley. 'I want one of those chocolate things,' he says.

Lawrie points and he's right. I have to admit, the Festive Yule Log Offer's pretty tempting. Lawrie's mother agrees.

'We'll have a Yule Log as well,' she says. '*And* some frozen éclairs.'

Top shoppers, or what? I'm warming to this lot already. Dad wanders off to the Wines and Spirits. I trail the others round the freezers. They're real shopaholics, I'm glad to say. By the time we reach the checkout the trolley's landsliding twelve-pack crisps, ham, mallows, jelly, Father Christmas-shaped novelty bars, oven chips, party-poppers, crackers, Bumper Nut Assortments, Country Baker mince pies, ready-to-roll icing, instant trifle mix, cake, pudding, mini-rolls, Festive Flavour Corn Puffs, Yule Log, sausage rolls plus two fat selection stockings. And *that's* just the stuff on top. Gross-out, or what? This is the family of my dreams.

I always *did* eat a lot. When I wasn't a ghost, I was fourteen. Then it was crisps, chips, biscuits, burgers, anything junky, okay? Now I'm a ghost, I feed on that special Christmas feeling of *never having enough* of whatever it was you really wanted. So you open all your presents, and the CD you got isn't right. The sweater someone bought you is *almost* right, except for the colour – are they *blind?* Plus your family's driving you mad. You wonder what Christmas is *for,* until Pictionary or Twister after dinner. Then the arguments start, and every other Christmas you ever remember comes flooding back with a bad taste, and instead of feeling sorry you feel spoiled and fed-up and ungrateful, like Christmas never gives you what you think it will, and somehow there must be more. That's what keeps me going. I always wanted *more.* Except every year, someone blows it. Sooner or later, someone does something nice or generous or heartwarming, and I'm gone. Can't stick that kind of thing.

Trolleys can tell you a lot. With a top trolley and no dates in sight – never bother haunting anyone with dates in their trolley, only sad people who never argue buy dates — the Bayleys make my day. I know they're called the Bayleys because I check out the credit card at the checkout. The squabble over the prawn crisps clinches it. The Battling Bayleys. I can feel it. I'm going to have a really joyful Christmas.

Kelly stuffs crisps and stares at me while her folks load up the car. You can get kids like this sometimes, the kind that's going to spot you right away. They tend to be a pain, except it doesn't matter too much what they say if they're little, because no one's going to believe they saw a ghost. Kelly's little. Six, maybe seven. I reckon it's a chance worth taking. I look back at the supermarket before we leave. *Ta-ra. Bye for now.* I've tried other stores, but you don't get the rush. Food shopping under pressure brings out the worst in people. I always come back to Super-Fare.

Okay, Christmas Eve with the Bayleys rates eight on the aggro scale. Enough bad vibes to snack off, not enough to pig out. I rove around the house for a while, sampling this room, then that. The kitchen tastes good to me. Mum unpacks the Christmas cake. She takes out the ready-rolled icing and gets it all stuck to her hands. Finally, she gets it on the cake. It looks like a badly-fitting nappy. She pulls out the cake decorations and sticks on trees and a reindeer. The Father Christmas figure won't stand up. She screws him into the cake so he's up to his knees in Special Offer Marzipan. She's getting pretty cross.

I'm enjoying myself quite a bit, when Dad throws a wobbler in the loft: 'Where did that thingie with the brass cherubs on it go? You know. The thing you light candles on, and the cherubs go round and round? What? *I'm not getting a thing about it.* I'd just like to find it one year, that's all.'

Dad comes downstairs and ruins his suede shoes dribbling hot UHT cream out of a Country Baker mince pie onto 'em. The kids watch a Christmas Eve ghost story on the telly. I have to tell you, the ghost in the story's pretty weak. If you're talking technique, I could show it a thing or two. Some ghosts go in for traditional stuff like busting mirrors, rapping on walls, turning lights and taps on and off, that kind of thing. Not me. I usually go for something simple but classy, like bending every clock hand in the house, crossing knives on the table, spelling out letters on the floor with whatever comes in handy, swapping keys around, etc., etc. Switch on the telly in the middle of the night and throw in a nightmare for the family dog, plus a pool of tomato ketchup on the settee, and you got 'em thoroughly spooked.

Anyway, Christmas Eve around midnight, I slip into Kelly Bayley's room in reverse Father Christmas mode. Usually what I do is, I take all the kids' Christmas presents out of their sacks and distribute them in weird places. It always throws 'em on Christmas morning, when they wake up and find things upside down in the hall or undone all over the floor and they realize nobody did it. It freaks 'em out every time. I've never known it fail.

Kelly's hit the jackpot this year. This year her Christmas sack's *huge.* Her parents have bought up every tacky plastic toy there *is,* plus they've left her *two* confectionary stockings. In front of everything else is Candy's House. Kelly's main present is Candy's House. I unwrap its pink-and-purple chimney. Candy's House is all pink-and-purple, and so is Candy's Stable and Candy's Styles, the hairdresser's shop with *real* shower-heads for *real* styles. I know these things, you see. I see them on TV. Kelly also has Poppy Pinhole, the Pocket-Sized Doll That's Your Friend. I stuff Poppy Pinhole down the chimney of Candy's House, and move on before I hurl.

Moving on down the sack, I take out a couple more presents. One of them feels like a game, the other's a soft toy or something, so I drift out and leave it in the bath. I unwrap its head. It's a soft-toy Dalmatian puppy, cute or what? I leave it leering down the toilet with a shaving foam hat on its head. Then I drift into the kitchen and stick a few knives in the wall. It's not very nice, I know, but how else can I let them know I want less Christmas spirit, more aggro? Good thing the dog's in the garage. I know it knows I'm there.

So I shimmy back into the bedroom and ghost out a few more toys. It's quite exciting, you know? It makes me feel quite nostalgic. I had presents, once. Once I had a bike on Christmas morning. That was before I got ill. I think about what I was like before I got ill. Then I get out the Bumper Smarties from Kelly's confectionary stocking and spell out

G – R – A – N – T

in Smarties all over Kelly Bayley's bedroom floor, because Grant was my name when I had Christmases. I don't have Christmases now. Only the sparks off other people's. I could get sorry for myself.

To cheer myself up a bit, I put a few things in the fridge – a Bat Ball, an Etch-a-Sketch and a pair of Glitter Leggings, and I hope they appreciate the joke. Back in the bedroom I spend quite a while balancing a board game over the door. Then just as I'm placing a Pink Pearl Bubble Bath on the very *edge* of the bookcase, I hear a noise in the bed. I look around. She's watching me. Kelly Bayley's awake.

'Those aren't *your* presents,' she says. 'Father Christmas left them for *me*.'

Ghosts never panic, OK? They can speak to you if they want to, it's just that most of them don't.

'Leave my presents *alone*,' she says. 'They're not for you, they're for me.'

I know that – I'm just helping.

'No, you're not,' she says, 'you're hiding things, you are.'

No, I'm not.

'You are.'

I'm putting them in funny places.

'Well, you shouldn't. You should go home.'

If only. *Home*, I think.

'You don't have a home, do you?' Kelly Bayley sits up and gives me the stare. 'I know who you are,' she says. 'You're the supermarket ghost.'

So? I send her, crushingly. What does she want, a medal?

'You needn't think –'

Needn't think what?

'You needn't think you're spoiling Christmas –'

Who's spoiling Christmas?

'– 'cos I won't *let* you.' She rubs her eyes. She's tired.

The Ghost of Christmas Shopping

Good. With luck, I hope, in the morning, she won't remember a thing.

I never did nothing, all right? I only moved a few things.

'I can see what you're doing. It's mean.'

It's only a joke, OK?

'Well, why don't you just stop *doing* it? Why don't you just go *away*?'

I don't usually get this kind of thing. It's pretty upsetting, actually. No one ever challenged me with those flashing brown eyes, the way Kelly Bayley does. With this kind of interference, the only thing to do is The Fade. I fade pretty quick, but is it *ever* a long time before she stops scouting the bedroom with those big brown eyes and finally goes back to sleep. By twelve forty-five I'm beginning to think the Bayleys may be my biggest mistake yet. I fade through the floor and rubbish the Christmas tree a bit, but it doesn't cheer me up as much as it usually does. For some reason.

'Tis the season to be jolly,
Tra-la-la-la-la-la Tra-la-la-la

Dad turns off the radio alarm. 'Happy Christmas, love.'

So it's Christmas morning and – BANG! – Kelly and Lawrie Bayley are *in* at their mum and dad's bedroom door and *all over* their mum and dad's bed with Christmas sacks and wrapping paper and tantrums, which is great, I mean, I'm *in*.

The first thing that happens is that Lawrie stands on his remote-control car. It's only his main present. He doesn't mean to. He didn't see it. He only just unwrapped it, and now it's *bro-oh-oh-ken*!

'And whose fault is that?' Dad says.

Lawrie's wail climbs higher and higher till Dad packs the car away and says he'll look at it later. He can look at it all he likes, it'll still be broken.

'It's broken an' *you* have to mend it!' Lawrie's spoilt tantrum explodes.

'I'll try to,' Dad says. 'Please.'

'An' you get your tool-box, please, an' you mend it *now*!'

'Lawrie,' Dad says, 'that will do.'

'Please. Can you. Mend it,' Lawrie huffs, through tears. 'Can you. Mend it. Now.'

'Not now, later,' Dad says. 'Open something else.'

'An'. You mend it. Now.'

He's really upset. I don't have to tell you, I'm enjoying

myself. Lawrie's sending out these barb-shaped selfish feelings I can puff myself up with to make myself bigger, stronger. Dad's hurt feelings give me back twice the energy I put out to make myself bigger. They don't even know they're doing it. It's a real Christmas breakfast. Enjoy.

Dad says, 'Shut *up,* Lawrie,' but Lawrie shuts up anyway, there's too many other things to open.

'COME-AN'-SEE-CANDY'S-HOUSE!' Kelly Bayley jumps up and runs in and out of her bedroom. Her mother follows her, laughing. 'AN'-HER-LIFT-GOES-UP-AN'-DOWN-IT-DOES SO-CAN-YOU-COME-AN'- *SEE*?'

Kelly's mother sees. In the meantime, Lawrie's batteries don't fit his Super Stunt Racetrack. Dad nips downstairs to feed the dog, so Lawrie forces in the batteries anyway, but they really don't want to go. Before Dad pounds back upstairs, Lawrie's trashed his Racetrack. The cars will never race round like they should, and no one will ever know why.

Mum reappears with Kelly. Kelly's well over the top. She *loves* her slippers and Art Deck, her videos and Slime Monsterz game. Most of all, she loves Candy's House, except someone went in the chimney.

'Someone went in the chimney?' Dad looks pretty crummy. He looks like he just saw a ghost.

'They really did!' Kelly covers her mouth. She can hardly speak for giggling. She makes it the *funniest* thing. 'Someone put Poppy Pinhole down Candy's chimney,' she gets out at last, 'and I'm going to go and *get* her!'

Dad's white as a sheet since he went downstairs. He looks like a ghost himself. Now he turns to Kelly Bayley's mother. 'Helen –' he says.

'What?' she says. 'Hey,' she says. She looks at him. 'Hey, what's up with you?'

'Something's strange – I don't know.'

'What?' she says. 'What's strange?'

'I went downstairs to feed, Nelson.' He takes a breath, and I know – don't you? – what's coming. 'I went downstairs to feed Nelson.' Another deep breath. 'And he wouldn't come into the kitchen. There's toys in the fridge, did you know? *And there's kitchen knives in the wall.*'

Kelly reappears in the doorway with Poppy Pinhole. 'Mum thinks I must've got up in the night, but I didn't,' she tells Poppy Pinhole.

Kelly looks up. She's uncertain. She puts her head on one side.

The Ghost of Christmas Shopping

'In my bedroom,' she says, 'why is there GRANT on the floor?'

I admit I've put them through it. I suppose you think I'm mean. I *am* mean, of course, that's the point. I'm not really dangerous, though, I'd just like to point out. Knives in the wall is as far as it goes with me. There *are* other ghosts I could mention – well, I could, but I won't.

So I make it through to dinnertime with the Bayleys. Almost half a Christmas day, it has to be some sort of record. Dinner's a real feast for me. I know I'm in for a treat when Lawrie looks at his sprouts.

'Eat up,' says Mum. 'It's only three sprouts. Think of all the people who haven't *got* any sprouts.'

Lawrie thinks. Then he says: 'An' *I* don't want any, either.'

'What's that?' says Dad. 'Just you think about all the people who haven't got any Christmas dinners at *all*.'

Lawrie goes red. Then he jumps up and huffs off upstairs. I just *hoover* up the bruised feelings afterwards. That's what I *call* Christmas dinner.

Old Lawrie doesn't come downstairs again until

quarter past two, by which time the pudding's well crusty. They *would* have to spoil everything and give him a cuddle. It's a dangerous moment, but it passes. Then they give him a choc-ice. Silly old sprouts, they say. Not worth getting upset about. Not on Christmas Day.

The afternoon's a bit so-so. A bit of aggro over telly schedules, nothing really tasty. Not that I mind after dinner. Dinner keeps me going until suppertime, no problem. By the time they're into the cold turkey sarnies, I don't mind admitting I'm a little peckish myself. I could do with a little resentment. I'm not fussy. A tiff would do, or an argument over a present – anything, really, to see me through till the Boxing Day niggles set in. I think I might be going to make it through a *whole Christmas Day* this time, I really do. All I need is a snack to keep me going. A scene before going to bed? That'll do nicely. Mum looks up at the clock once or twice, but Kelly Bayley ignores her. Bum in the air, she's playing a game. No one's put her to bed until now. She's done pretty well, keeping quiet.

Mum clears her throat. 'Kelly.'

I'm waiting to see what'll happen. There's got to be something in this for me. It could be just what I need.

The Ghost of Christmas Shopping

'Look at the time.' Mum gets up. 'Kelly, did you hear me?'

Dad says, 'Come on, Kelly, time for bed.'

Kelly frowns. 'Can't I stay up? *Please?*'

'You *have* stayed up. It's nine o'clock. Enough excitement for one day.'

'But I just want to do my Zoo Quiz one more time. Just only one more –'

'Kelly.' Dad looks up.

Kelly Bayley opens her mouth. She's about to make a scene. Then she looks at me. She looks at me, and she *knows*.

Then you know what she does? Instead of stamping and crying and flushing and sending out sparks I can use, she does *completely the reverse*. Kelly Bayley looks at me the way she looked at me in her bedroom the night before Christmas. Then she goes up to Mum in her stupid panda slippers and her dumb-looking glitter wig and her brand-new Christmas nightdress, and you know what she says?

She says, 'Thanks for Christmas Day, Mum. It was *brilliant*.'

'Well, it's been a funny old Christmas Day.'

I'll say. They only searched the house from top to

bottom, Mum and Dad, and then they put away all the knives and anything else sharp you could cut with. At least it brought them together at Christmas time. That's the way I look at it, anyway.

'Thanks for all my presents,' Kelly Bayley says, 'and for everything else, *ever*. You're my *best* Mum and Dad.'

You're my *best* Mum and Dad. Can you believe that? Thanks for Christmas Day, Mum. It was *brilliant*. And old Kelly Bayley, she kisses her mother goodnight. And Mum hugs her tight, eyes closed, folding her warm in her arms. And – thanks, Kelly Bayley – I'm gone.

Families. It happens every year. Sooner or later, they get to you with some gen-u-ine love and warmth. There's no stopping them. What would a Christmas without warmth be? It'd be, well – cold. Like me. Pretty soon now I'll be climbing back into my freezer. Soon I'll be frozen stiff, well out of it till next year's happy shoppers come to warm me up. It doesn't usually bother me. But this year, I think it might.

Right now, the supermarket's dead. All the aisles are cold and dark and empty. The plastic strip-curtain by the deli counter clacks a bit in the draught. The checkouts loom at the far end like the keys of some piano no one plays any more. I picture the once-feverish Christmas shoppers, home now with Grade-A headaches and a nagging feeling that the guarantee for the joystick someone stood on went out in the bin with the wrapping paper. Christmas. Why can't it be simple?

I wouldn't mind, but they never learn. They'll do it all again, just the same, next year. The last week before Christmas they'll be back in their droves in panic mode, scrabbling for frozen turkeys in my freezer, waking me up, as usual, when shopping fever peaks. I start wondering about them all, hoping everyone got what they really deserved this Christmas. Then I pull myself up. What am I, the Christmas fairy?

I count cut-price offers for a while. Then I start thinking about Kelly Bayley. I wish I could stop, but I can't. *You needn't think you're spoiling Christmas*, she says. *It's mean*, she says. *Why don't you just stop doing it?* And her brown eyes scout me up and down.

Maybe she's right. Maybe I *should* stop doing it. Why be a mean ghost when I could be the Ghost of Family Feeling? The Ghost of Icky Moments? The Ghost of Going-To-Bed-Nicely? Right now, I'm thinking maybe a change of diet next Christmas mightn't be so bad.

I may just try chewing on a little goodwill-to-all, why not? Not as good as ice-cream. But probably better than sour grapes, whatever *they* taste like. I picture Kelly Bayley snuggling down in bed, glitter wig stowed on the lamp-stand so she spots it first thing in the morning. I picture her waking up, clapping it on, rushing downstairs in her dressing-gown for Boxing Day cartoons. Hey, Kelly Bayley, you've got me thinking I've changed. No kidding. Can I come Christmas Day next year? See you in your brand-new smartypants outfit? With your next year's novelty slippers snapping on your feet? And stick around till midnight, even, like I never did before? Would you let me, Kelly Bayley? I promise I wouldn't eat too much. I'd do anything you tell me.

So, that's about it for this year. Nothing lonelier than a supermarket at midnight on the twenty-fifth of December, so I might as well pack up right now. The freezer sighs as I open the lid. *My* freezer. The freezer I was looking in when I haemorrhaged. When I was fourteen. When I was Christmas shopping. With Mum. I died on the way to hospital. But I found my way back straightaway. Been hanging around ever since. The Ghost of Christmas Shopping. I tell you, it almost frightens *me*.

Stuff Police

The day he borrowed his brother Aran's bike and carelessly left it propped against the dustbins overnight was a very special day for Justin Needham. He didn't know it at the time. But next morning, he pretty soon knew it. Next morning Justin Needham looked out of his bedroom window and felt ever so slightly sick. The reason was the dustmen. And what the dustmen had done. Or what the dustmen had *taken*, to be precise.

Oh, no! The bin-men had been! Aran's bike – where was it???

They'd taken his brother Aran's mountain bike. The mountain bike he, Justin Needham, had had special dispensation to borrow for *only one evening*. He'd only left it out the front – against the bins, admittedly. How *could* they have taken it away? What were they, stupid? Couldn't the dustmen *see* it hadn't been put out with the rubbish, even though it looked as if it had? The whole horrendous situation flashed on Justin Needham in an instant. It wasn't a new bike, admittedly. It looked pretty scuzzy and old. The dustmen *did* take big items away. Plus, he'd thrown the bike down by the bins last night as his dad had been putting them out. He'd meant to go back and put it away. He hadn't known *this* would happen.

Slowly the scale of what actually *had* happened percolated through the brain of Justin Needham. Aran wasn't going to like it. Aran was large and peevish. He especially liked his well-used and customized mountain bike. He rode it most weekends. Today was Friday. Friday Trials up Mine Trax was a popular event. Aran would want his mountain bike as soon as he got in from work. 'Chain it round the front when you've finished,' Aran had said, when he, Justin, had begged to borrow his, Aran's, bike the previous night. 'I'm going up Engels' tomorrow. So make sure it's round the front.'

Aran meant Terry Engels. He and Terry Engels and

Stuff Police

Simon 'Madman' Madeley rode up on the mine most Friday nights and thrashed around in the silt, one reason Aran's bike looked like a tank had driven over it. Now, probably, a tank – or a JCB – *would* drive over Aran's bike. At the dump.

Or the yard. Wherever they took these things. Justin Needham swallowed. This was big. He'd only forgotten to put a *bike* away. The consequences of his *not* having put the stupid bike away were, like, out of all proportion. This was like forgetting to pick up your sandwiches and starting the Third World War. *Chain it round the front when you've finished*. He'd left it round the front, all right. It was just that he'd forgotten to chain it. Forgotten to prop it against the wall. Forgotten all about it. He'd really blown it this time. So he had a rep for leaving things – stuff, mainly – for leaving *stuff* lying around. This was something special. No one would give him a chance to explain. It would be so *typical* of him.

Justin Needham pressed his face to the window and looked up and down the road. The dustbin lids lay where the bin-men had thrown them down in their neck-breaking rush to get through their rounds and off for their elevenses. Hang on a minute. One of the lids was still spinning – the bin men had only just gone!

Brainstorms

Justin Needham flung himself down the stairs and into the road outside. 'Hey,' he shouted, 'excuse me?' he raced to the corner. *'Please wait!'*

But the dustmen were long gone. Long gone, too, was any last glimpse of Aran's bike. Justin sat down on the pavement. What now? he wondered. Another bike? *By two o'clock in the afternoon, when Aran finished his shift?* Aran hadn't even left for work yet. Justin got up and dusted off his hands. He had to keep it together until Aran had left the house. He'd think about replacement bikes, or whatever, with Aran safely out of the way on the early shift at Kingburger.

So where *did* the dustmen take things? Justin had never actually thought about it before. He tried hard and pictured a rubbish dump at the end of the world under a bloody red sunset. He pictured his brother's bike collapsing under a crusher, its sad remaining components picked over and splatted by gulls. How could this have *happened*? To him, Justin Needham? Maybe he should just tell Aran and get it over with. Justin pictured telling Aran his bike had been taken away. Then he lidded the bins and took them in.

'Nice work, Justin,' his father said. 'And while you're at it you can bring in that stuff in the garden.'

Justin sighed. 'OK.' So he left things lying around sometimes. What was it? Crime of the century?

Then he had an inspiration. 'You didn't bring Aran's bike in last night?'

'No. Why?'

'I just thought you might've brought it in.'

'Why are you asking me?'

'No problem,' Justin lied. 'I just thought you might have moved it.'

'You didn't tidy your room last night?'

'No, but I thought about it.'

He didn't feel like breakfast. But Justin ate some anyway. His father got ready to run Aran to work. After he'd run Aran to work he'd come home and gripe at Justin, unless Justin got out of his way. Justin's dad worked from home. That's what he called it, working from home. But mainly he worked from the armchair in the living room where he sat and watched telly most days.

Aran put his head round the door. 'Hey, Bungle, what did I say?'

'What did you say about what?'

Aran called Justin 'Bungle' sometimes. There wasn't a lot he could do.

'My bike, duffo. Round the front. Didn't you get what I said?'

Justin's nerve-endings tingled. *Hey, pizza-brain, it's down the dump. Try riding it after that.* 'It's round the back,' he lied, coolly. 'I'll get it in a minute.'

'Just so it's there when I get in from work.' Aran put on his Kingburger hat. 'See you later, losers.'

The car coughed out of the driveway and chugged away up the road. Justin waited a moment or two, then wandered up to the lay-by where the bin-men sometimes pulled in for a fag and a Thermos, on the off-chance he'd see or hear them. He walked crisply back with the din of birds in his ears and neither sight nor sound of the dustcart with its straining jaws chewing up the stuff people had fed it, and the dirty old dolls and teddy-bears the dustmen had rescued from the rubbish bobbing sadly along in front.

'What happens, you know, when the dustmen take things away?' Justin asked his father, when he'd got back.

'They take it down the dump.'

'Then what?'

'Some of it gets recycled.' Justin's father shrugged. 'Some of it gets sent away.'

'Where does it get sent away to?'

'The landfill site, I think. Most of it goes there to start with.'

'What about big things, though? Things like –'

'Washing machines? Bound to get recycled.'

What about bikes? Justin wanted to say. *Especially bikes taken away by mistake.* He pictured Aran's mountain bike getting recycled. Then he said: 'They don't get melted down, or anything?'

'Probably. How would I know?'

Justin digested this. Then he said, 'They might probably take things home?'

'Who?'

'The dustmen? If someone throws something away, and it's still, like, really good? Like a bike or a cooker or something?'

'They might, I suppose, I don't know.' Justin's dad shook out the paper and sat down with it in a don't-bother-me-any-more kind of way. 'Why all this interest in dustmen?'

Justin had another inspiration. 'Where *is* the dump?' he asked.

'Curtain Road, I suppose,' his father said. 'Look it up in the phone book. And pick up that stuff on the stairs while you're at it. It's been there at least three days.'

Justin looked it up. *County Environmental Services*, the phone book said. *Curtain Road Recycling Centre, Open Six Days a Week*. Curtain Road was in Moorstock, some seven or eight miles away. How to get there to find a bike, with no bike to get there *on*?

'Have you picked up that stuff on the stairs yet?' his father asked him.

'Just going out, but I will.'

'How about the stuff in the garden?'

Justin dodged out before his father could get into it. So what if he left stuff lying around on the stairs? What was it, a few socks or schoolbooks? Pick this up, pick that up. A few little things on the floor, and Dad got out of his pram. He was over-compensating, probably. Trying to prove he could run the house and look after two boys as *well* as being unemployed. He hadn't been the same since he lost his job. His father should get out more. Move *this* stuff, move *that* stuff – what was he, the *stuff police*?

Justin Needham took the eleven-ten bus to Moorstock and sallied out onto Curtain Road at about eleven forty-five. Curtain Road was a long road, which wound its way past Justin's school – closed now, for the holidays – before licking off out to Magwell Crags and the river-meanders beyond *that*. Justin checked the closed-up doors and windows, the silent school halls and playing fields, with enormous satisfaction. Easter holidays. Way to go. Two and a half weeks of glorious freedom, and no one to tell you how to use it or make you feel bad you hadn't handed in something complicated they'd dreamed up for you to do, just so they could sit on it for three months before handing it back for you to mark yourself, in the interests of Self Assessment. It was so stupid. How do you feel you've coped with this project? Brilliantly, of course. How many marks do I give myself? A* plus three million, plus an honours degree and a silver cup – what did you *think* I'd give myself? A raspberry?

Justin slowed. CURTAIN ROAD RECYCLING CENTRE, said the sign. OPEN SIX DAYS A WEEK.

So here he was at the dump. So why was he so nervous? Of course they'd realize his brother's bike'd been brought there by mistake, if he explained it. It wouldn't be, like, the only mistake in the *world*. It was easy to explain – wasn't it? *Good morning, you know you handle large items? Well, I'm looking for a black Snakebite*

Brainstorms

Series 2 mountain bike, pretty beat up – oh, right, it came in this morning? Yeah – a mistake, too right – that's brilliant, thanks a lot. Another five minutes, and it would've gone in the crusher? My lucky day? No kidding. Probably it would go easily. Probably he'd be out and away in five minutes. Probably things got taken away by mistake all the time. Probably he'd better go in.

Justin wandered in. The roar of a reversing caterpillar-track crane, straining to pull something almost too large for it out of a pile of scrap-metal, took the words right out of his mouth as he tried, at least three times, to explain what he was looking for to the strange-looking man in the tin shed by the entrance. The strange-looking man in the tin shed by the entrance just narrowed his eyes and nodded, whatever Justin said, and pointed down to the dump. Justin was pretty sure he hadn't heard a thing. He had an impressive collection of broken clocks in his shed. Justin wondered what he did with them. Probably he tried to get them going.

A dumb row of broken washing machines lined the lane down to the main dump and the landfill beyond. Justin's spirits rose. He couldn't help but notice one or two bikes in amongst the rolls of old carpet and noxious old settees. This was the Large Items dump. It held everything from hot-water tanks to wardrobes, dishwashers, fridges, tumble-driers, rotting beds and mattresses, push-chairs and broken office equipment, anything, in fact, too large to sink in the landfill, with some reclaimable parts. So far, so good. All he had to do now was find out where the dustcarts came in. And what had come in that morning. Twelve o'clock. The dustcart must have come in by *now*. Probably it was out on the landfill, where all the gulls were wheeling. But would it have checked into Large Items first to off-load Aran's bike? The man in the tin shed must know.

Justin almost turned back to ask him. But it was no use. He'd never make Tin Shed understand. Tin Shed's mind had been blunted by staying too long at the dump. No wonder, when the dump was a nightmare. Never, Justin thought, never had he seen so much *stuff*. No wonder Tin Shed had gone a bit strange with so much *stuff* building up round his shed, so that his shed grew darker and darker and might even disappear some day under the odds and ends and Large Items of *other people's lives*.

'Looking for something?'

'I'm sorry?' Justin spun round. A tall man. In grey. Behind him. Where had *he* sprung from? he wondered.

'I said, are you looking for something?' the stranger repeated.

Justin Needharn stared. 'Um. I don't think – not really.'

The man in the grey coat nodded. 'Anything you want here. You only have to look.'

'I didn't know dumps were like this,' Justin said.

The man in the grey coat looked at him. 'What did you think they were like?'

Justin walked back down the lane. He would ask Tin Shed where the dustcarts came in. Then he would find Aran's bike. Then he would get off home, and be in before two o'clock.

'I live in the house down the road,' the stranger said, falling in beside Justin. 'Want to come back and see it?'

'Not really,' Justin said edgily. 'I just want my brother's bike.'

The stranger stopped. 'Is it a Snakebite Series 2? Handlebars a bit twisted?'

'That's the one.' Justin's heart almost stopped. 'Did you – have you seen it?'

'Fifteen gears?'

'Right.'

'Alloy rims? Water bottle and cage?'

'Check.'

'Carbon steel frame, the worse for wear?'

'Whatever – have you seen it?'

'Seen it?' The stranger smiled. 'I rescued it this morning.'

'You rescued it this morning?' Glorious, golden words. Justin had to repeat them.

'I thought it might be a mistake. It's only round the corner. Back with the rest of my stuff.'

'It was an accident, see?' Relief flooded Justin's voice. This man had Aran's bike. He was going to get it back. His chest eased at last. He became quite confidential. 'My brother, see, he lent me his bike, because well, you don't want to know –'

'Yes, I do,' the stranger said. 'Why don't we get it while you tell me?'

'– and my dad, he's always saying, why don't you pick up your stuff? So next time, I probably will. Put away Aran's bike, I mean, else he'll kill me. But it's funny how things just pile up, and the next thing you know there's just *millions* –'

'Tell me about it,' Lomax said. 'See all the stuff around *here*?'

Justin drank his tea and looked around. The man in grey wasn't a stranger any more, after all.

He was the man with Aran's bike at his house, name of Lomax. That was how Justin Needham squared going home with a stranger. Lomax watched him squaring it. Once they were in at his garden gate, he gave Justin time to settle. He let him look around the yard. He even invited him in.

'Come in,' Lomax said, 'why don't you?'

'I can't,' Justin said. 'I shouldn't.'

'The name's Lomax,' Lomax said. 'And you are?'

'Just going,' said Justin.

'I'll get your brother's bike,' Lomax said, 'if you give me half a tick. Come in a bit and sit down,' he said, 'it's not as if you don't know me. Not now we've been introduced.'

Justin sneezed. 'It's dusty.'

'It's this stuff,' Lomax said. 'It owns me. I can't even *give* it away.'

Lomax wasn't kidding. His house and yard and garden groaned with stuff brought home from the dump – dusty, useless, dog-eared stuff, stuff no one would willingly lumber themselves with if they could bring themselves to throw it away. Bikes and baths; carpets and car-parts; chicken-coops and chairs; pig-arks and prams; pews and mangles and harrows and blocks and dressers and tellies and half a fairground ride – or, at least, the cars off the ride. Plus a washing-line hung entirely with old leather gloves, and a stack of timber and roof tiles that ran all the way down to the car-hulks along by the wall. The wall itself was hung with mole-traps. Beyond that stood an old chaise-longue settee, and beyond *that* a whole half-a-boat.

Inside Lomax's house, the stuff had settled. There had been plenty of time – bags and bags of time – for *stuff* to settle into every corner under a thick layer of dust. Pots and pans and stags' heads; brollies and skeletons and tailor's dummies; stuffed quails and carriage-clocks; fire-irons and ice-picks; butterflies and butter-pats; comics and motorbike parts; lava lamps and leaping salmon in not-so-leaping glass cases; monkey wrenches and socket-sets; boxes of cogs and badges, screws and grommets and washers; sink-plungers and sump oil; bottles and boots and bags and shoes and hats and *windowsills* full of frosted mineral quartzes and seashells fuzzed with dust – all the *stuff* of the world had settled in nicely at Lomax's house and got its feet under the table. It had made itself quite at home. Unlike Justin Needham.

Justin was staying a *minute*, that was all. Lomax was weird but OK, plus the door stood open – plus he needed the bike. He hadn't actually *seen* Aran's bike. Lomax would get it in a minute.

'Take a seat while I get the bike,' Lomax had said, opening the door. 'I'm done in, how about you?'

He *looked* done in, Justin thought, with his grey-looking skin and his tired eyes and his fumbling, fiddling fingers. Lomax had shrugged off his coat to put on the kettle. Under his grey coat he wore a grey cardigan over grey-looking trousers. Everything he had on was grey. The house was grey, as well. Justin looked around. Strange growths and lumps grew out of the walls and stairs. It took Justin a moment to realise they were only things covered in dust. Most dust, Justin remembered from something he'd read, most dust was *dead human skin cells*.

'How do you like your tea?'

Justin stared. '*Like* it?'

'Black or white?' Lomax asked. 'With milk or without?'

'With, thanks.' *No dead skin cells, thanks.* 'I shouldn't do this,' Justin said. 'I shouldn't even *be* here.'

'You're right,' Lomax said, making tea. 'It's never OK to do this. Sugar, or do you want biscuits?'

'This is, like, what my dad would think is horrible.' Justin meant the rubbish-covered garden outside the still-open front door. 'I don't,' he added quickly, 'but my dad would.'

'It's like what I think is horrible. I'm trapped, see?' Lomax swirled the teapot round and round. 'A prisoner of all this stuff. Can't get rid of it. Can't leave it. Completely stuffed, that's me.'

Justin changed the subject. 'Is that the time already?'

A row of fluffy grey clocks on the fluffy grey mantelpiece agreed it was twelve forty-five. He would need a good hour to cycle Aran's bike home before Aran got in and wanted it. He'd need to set out pretty soon.

'My parents said they'd leave me if I didn't clear up my stuff.' Lomax poured the tea. 'That was a long time ago.'

'That's a bit strong,' Justin said.

'I can make it weaker.'

'Your folks, I mean, not the tea.'

'When they said they'd leave me?' Lomax added milk to Justin's tea. The tea was grey like his face. 'Know what happened? They did.'

'They left you? Because you were *untidy*?'

'"Leave me alone" I told them. "Let me live my own life".'

Justin swallowed. 'And did they?'

'What do *you* think?' Lomax laughed sarcastically. 'What do you think all *this* is?'

All *what*? Justin's heart hammered. The lumps on the stairs – what *were* they? They looked like piles of books. A dust-covered guitar. Long-dead plants, a sweater in holes, a frisbee. Records, magazines, schoolbooks. How long had they *been* there? Were these – *Lomax's schoolbooks*?

'"Get off my back" I told them,' Lomax went on. '"So I don't put stuff away – what are you, the Stuff Police?"'

Justin got up. He felt sick. 'I have to go,' he said. This man had looked inside his mind. Or *the Stuff Police had got him*.

'I told them straight – "So I don't put stuff away for *ten years*, so what?"'

'So you didn't?' Justin said.

'What?'

94

Stuff Police

'Put stuff away for ten years?'

'I *never* put stuff away,' Lomax said. 'See that jigsaw in the corner? I did that in nineteen seventy-four.'

'Excuse me,' Justin said. 'I have to go to the bathroom.'

'Down the hall.' Lomax pointed. 'First door on your left.'

First door on your left. Justin's heart hammered. This strange house. This strange morning. Lomax was freaking him out. Soon – when? – he would go and fetch Aran's bike. Or maybe he wouldn't. *Maybe he never meant to.* Justin gasped for breath. His chest felt like it would burst. He'd leg it out of the bathroom window if he possibly could, tell his dad about the bike, and come back for it later. That was the one. *Out, out, out!* Enough weird things already. Justin followed the dank and smelly corridor, past busts and prints and posters, until the tips of his fingers told him he'd reached the first door on his left.

As soon as the door swung open, he knew there was no way out. The windows in Lomax's bathroom were solid with rust and dirt. The basin and toilet were orange with rust. A fly swam in the pan. There was no escape.

There would be nothing for it but to front his way out. Justin wasn't sure he could do it.

Justin Needham re-entered the room briskly.

'OK,' he said brightly. He rubbed his hands. 'Let's go and get that bike.'

'I tried to escape once,' Lomax went on, as though Justin had never gone out. 'Twice, in fact, the last time twelve years ago.'

'See, I've got to ride home straightaway,' Justin said, ignoring him. 'Before my brother gets in. It should take me thirty, forty minutes. Forty-five minutes, tops.' Justin checked his watch. 'So can we get the bike, now? If that's OK with you?'

'The first time I tried to escape I was only about your age. Know what I found when I came back?'

'No,' Justin said. 'What?'

'My parents had moved away. They'd left me most of their stuff.'

'What?' Justin said. 'All this?'

'I had to stay and look after it. The stuff wouldn't let me go. I lived alone and nothing changed for years and years and years. But one day, someone came and took my place.' Lomax got up and circled the room. 'The second time I escaped, I stayed away. Merchant seaman for ten years. No room for *stuff* on board ship. I came back two years ago. It's all just the way I left it.' Lomax picked up a book off the stairs. He brushed it off and smiled. 'Outlands Comprehensive, Biology, Miss Smart.' He looked at Justin Needham. 'The stuff on the stairs was covered in dust and right where I left it when I was thirteen, thirty-three years ago.'

Justin stared. 'No kidding.'

'Now I can't get away, you see. I can't just get up and leave it.'

'My mum's just the opposite.' Justin cleared his throat. Lomax wasn't so bad. With parents like that, it wasn't his fault he was weird. 'My mum, she throws things away as soon as they hit ground. She throws stuff away all the time.'

'Ah yes, the Thrower Away,' Lomax put his fingertips together. 'Let me tell you something. There's Hoarders and Ditchers in this world – that's Throwers Away, like your mum.'

'Which am I?' Justin asked.

'You're like me,' Lomax said. 'You're just like I was at your age.'

Thirty-three years ago, Lomax had thrown down his schoolbooks. That made him young in the sixties. Justin looked around. Lava lamps and posters, magazines and records and a circular plastic chair jumped out in a sixties way. He'd even had a model Dalek from *Doctor Who* – original version. He'd added to it, since them. But the room was like Lomax's time capsule. A capsule that wouldn't let him go.

'Wondering how I got so much *stuff* in the first place?' Lomax asked.

'Not really,' Justin said. '*I must go.*'

'I never tidied my room, see, when I was a kid. I didn't pick stuff up because I didn't think it mattered. My parents did it for me.' Lomax rounded on Justin. 'But let me tell you, boy, stuff has a way of just *lying down on top of you* and clogging up your life. My parents were right, I know now. But I had to learn it the hard way – at the dump.'

'I'm going now,' Justin said.

'I wanted to go, too, but I couldn't,' Lomax said. 'I couldn't get clear of my *stuff* you see. I'm still not clear of it now.'

'So,' Justin said, 'my brother's bike.'

'So. Your brother's bike.' But Lomax made no move to get it. 'Like a bar of chocolate for the journey?' He rummaged in his pocket. 'These Picnics aren't too bad.

I've had 'em since the sixties.'

'Pass.' Justin said. 'Have you tried UFOs? They're lush.'

'UFOs. I've seen 'em.' Lomax unwrapped a Picnic.

'What's your name?' Justin asked, after a moment.

'Name's Lomax. I told you.'

'What's your first name, though?'

'I used to be Justin Lomax. But that was before I had *stuff.* Now I have nothing but trouble, see? Nothing makes me happy.'

Justin? Justin *Lomax?* The smile fell from Justin's face. He had to pretend he hadn't heard. Weird alarms rang all over. *Now's the time. Get out.* In his confusion, he said, 'Nothing makes you happy? Is that why you took the bike?'

'I didn't take it, I rescued it.'

'So can we get it now?'

Nothing, see? Nothing makes me happy. Everything seemed grey in this house of dust, a house once policed by the Stuff Police, now empty of any feeling except loss and the wish to escape.

'Escape,' breathed the books on the stairs.

'Escape,' whispered the mouldering old palms by the window and the mouldering old hats on the hat-stand, the bags and shoes and bottles, the kinky boots by the door. Escape, escape, escape . . .

'The bike?' Justin insisted.

'Right now?'

'Please.'

'Yes,' said Lomax, 'well, then.'

'Time to go,' Justin said. 'Sorry, it's just that I'm late.'

'It is, indeed, time to go,' Lomax sprang up quite suddenly. 'Follow me, then,' he said. 'You'd better put on this coat.'

'Why do I need a coat?'

'The bike,' Lomax said, 'it's in the cellar.' And he draped his grey coat around Justin. 'You'll need this, too,' Lomax said, and he put his grey hat on Justin's head.

'Just a minute,' Justin said, 'I don't need stuff like this.'

'Oh,' said Lomax, 'I think you do,' and he wheeled out Justin's brother's bike from behind a cupboard door.

'It's not in the cellar at *all*,' Justin said. 'Why didn't you tell me it was there?'

Lomax pushed wide the cluttered front door and the uncluttered sunlight flooded in. One thirty-five, said the line of grey clocks over the grey and ash-choked fireplace. Just twenty-five minutes to cycle home before Aran gets in, Justin thought. He could just about make it if he killed himself. But how could he leave all this stuff?

Lomax cocked a leg over Justin Needham's brother's bike. 'So long,' he said. 'It's all yours now.'

'What d'you mean – all mine?'

'All this *stuff* – be seeing you.' And Lomax rode out into the sunshine.

'Wait!' Justin cried. 'That's not your bike! Come back!' he cried. '*Mr Lomax!*'

But Lomax peddled off like a madman, down the road, past the dump, down Curtain Road to the school. And as he went he seemed to grow smaller, younger. His back grew narrower, his legs shorter – he seemed bullet-headed, somehow. Like a boy. A boy on a bike.

'*Hey, Lomax – Lomax, come back!*'

He looked like any other boy would look by the time he drew abreast of the school. Justin Needham rubbed his eyes. His fingers were dirty and grey. He went into the house. He looked in the mirror. 'Mr Lomax?' he said. 'Is that you?'

Brainstorms

It wasn't Justin Needham. It wasn't Justin Needham who put on the grimy kettle in the dirty, dust-filled kitchen. Who sat down in the dirty grey chair. Justin Needham had gone. Gone? It wasn't Justin Needham who looked – again and again – in the mirror. Who clutched his grey face with his hands. Who understood he was trapped, a prisoner of all this stuff. He couldn't get rid of it, and he couldn't leave it, *unless someone else took his place* – and who would want to do that?

Justin Lomax brewed his tea and slept in his dirty grey bed, with the stuff of the dump all around him. He could never leave this place. The Stuff Police wouldn't let him. They couldn't make him pick stuff up any more. But they wouldn't let him throw it away. He would never see Aran come home from work. Never come home from school again, and see Dad's pinched-looking face make a smile, where making a smile was an effort. He would bide his time. Some other person who never put stuff away was bound to come along sooner or later. Until then, he could wait.

If he listened *very carefully* he could hear the sound of falling dust. Of slowly gathering skin cells – *his* dead skin cells – slowly falling around him. Lomax picked up a dirty grey record off the stairs. *With the Beatles*, the title read. Lomax looked at the sleeve. Then he opened the lid on an ancient record player. He'd be with the Beatles a long time. He might as well hear them sing.

If you've recovered from

Brainstorms

look out for more Tales from a Sick Bed . . .

L. P. HOWARTH

WARNING, SERIOUSLY WEIRD!

Tales from a Sick Bed

The Medicine Chest

A very weird bug is going around

You know when you're ill in bed, and everything looks larger than life, kind of super-real and out-of-scale, as though something as big as a gorilla in the wardrobe is about to reveal itself?

Open the Medicine Chest!

Warning! Read these stories and the world will never look the same again.

L. P. HOWARTH
WARNING, SERIOUSLY WEIRD!
Tales from a Sick Bed
REPTILON
Fever Dreams
when feverish thoughts invade your brain

You know when you are off school and ill in bed and everything seems kind of large and nightmarish – when feverish thoughts invade your brain, and you're not sure where they come from?

You're having a Fever Dream!

Warning! Read these stories and the world will never look the same again.

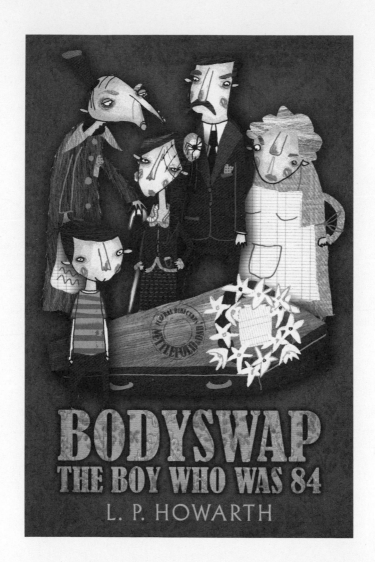

BODYSWAP
THE BOY WHO WAS 84

L. P. HOWARTH

And don't miss
Bodyswap The Boy who was 84

Will Dudgeon is thirteen years old when his body
is stolen by a century-hopping villain. Suddenly
Will's the oldest man he's ever seen (with all the
aches and pains that go with that).

At least he's inherited the right job. As assistant at
Nettlefold and Dad Funeral Directors, Will can
offer really wicked, wedged, full-on, top-dog,
superfine funerals, best and plushest on the terrace!

But for how long? Can Will persuade the dastardly
Hornbeam to give him his young body back or
will his next funeral be his own?